MAY 3 1

# THE
# SHELF-PAPER
# JUNGLE

## DIANA ENGEL

MACMILLAN PUBLISHING COMPANY    NEW YORK
MAXWELL MACMILLAN CANADA    TORONTO
MAXWELL MACMILLAN INTERNATIONAL    NEW YORK    OXFORD    SINGAPORE    SYDNEY

FOR

DEBBIE

AND

ANNA

With a special thanks to
Eve Holwell and Luisa Engel

Copyright © 1994 by Diana Engel
All rights reserved. No part of this book may be reproduced or transmitted in any form or by any means, electronic or mechanical, including photocopying, recording, or by any information storage and retrieval system, without permission in writing from the Publisher. Macmillan Publishing Company is part of the Maxwell Communication Group of Companies. Macmillan Publishing Company, 866 Third Avenue, New York, NY 10022. Maxwell Macmillan Canada, Inc., 1200 Eglinton Avenue East, Suite 200, Don Mills, Ontario M3C 3N1.
First edition
Printed in the United States of America
The text of this book is set in 16 pt. Usherwood Medium.
The illustrations are rendered in pen-and-ink, watercolor, and colored pencil.
1   3   5   7   9   10   8   6   4   2

Library of Congress Cataloging-in-Publication Data
Engel, Diana. The shelf-paper jungle / written and illustrated by Diana Engel. —
1st ed.      p.      cm. Summary: Two little girls create a whole world of their own—a
jungle on a roll of shelf paper. ISBN 0-02-733464-3   [1. Friendship-Fiction.   2. Jungles—Fiction.   3. Drawing—
Fiction.]   I. Title.   PZ7.E69874Sh   1994          [E]—dc20          93-21772

Lila and Frannie were best friends. They had been best friends for as long as they could remember.

Through good times and bad times, rain or shine, Lila and Frannie's friendship grew.

One cold afternoon in the middle of winter, the girls
looked for some drawing paper in a big kitchen drawer at
Lila's house.

"Let's use this," said Frannie, holding up the remains of a
roll of shelf paper.

Upstairs, in Lila's room, they let the roll unwind. The long, white paper stretched beyond their reach, like a snow-covered path, calling them to follow.

"What shall we make?" asked Lila.

"Hmmm," said Frannie. "How about some trees…and some birds…and maybe some flowers?"

"And some animals," said Lila. "And bugs and—"

"A jungle!" they both shouted.

The two friends worked for a long, long time. The white paper soon filled with shapes and lines and, most of all, color.

"Let's do this again tomorrow," said Lila. "Come over after school." She carefully rolled up the paper and put it in her pajama drawer.

"This is our secret now," said Frannie. "We'll work on it till the whole roll is done!"

Lila and Frannie got together many times to work on their secret jungle, and through the seasons, they spent long afternoons drawing and painting.

As time passed, the paper roll grew more and more beautiful, filled with every creature imaginable, and bursting with color.

One day in early summer, Frannie arrived at Lila's looking
terrible.

"What happened? What's the matter?" Lila asked. Frannie
began to cry. "We're moving away," she sputtered. "I'm
going to a new school in September!"

Lila joined her friend on the bed. They both sobbed.

That summer, Lila and Frannie were inseparable. They knew their time together was rushing by.

On the day before the big move, Lila and Frannie took out their secret jungle. "Let's cut it in half," said Frannie, "and we'll each take a piece."

Sadly, they unrolled their shelf-paper jungle and weighted each end with books. At the end of their unfinished work, a space of white paper remained. The rest was a bright, rich carpet full of all the afternoons they had shared happily, side by side.

The girls stood motionless, staring at the bright colors.
The longer they stared, the bigger and bigger the jungle
became and the smaller and smaller they felt.

It was as if they could smell the richness of the jungle:
damp, earthy, and flower-sweet. Could they hear squawking
and rustling and chirping and buzzing? Did every creature
stretch and yawn?

Lila grabbed Frannie's hand. They ran, laughing, through their own green world.

Together they danced beneath blooms as big as trees and

slid down palms where candy-colored snakes hung like streamers.

They ate bananas and scratched like two itchy monkeys,

and flew on the back of a huge striped bird…

in and out and all around their steamy, dreamy, secret jungle

through moonlight and starlight and in between…

and landed—*plop!*—in the middle of a green-blue sea

filled with turtles and frogs and fabulous fish and...

alligators! Run!

Faster and faster they ran, onto the tail…

of a sleeping lion! He roared a monstrous roar that sent the girls

scrambling, up, up, up to the top of the tallest tree,

where they rested, cooled by silent wings.

Frannie saw two curly vines and nudged Lila.
They both reached out, grabbed hold, and swung…

out over the sleeping hippos,

past the flamingos, beak to beak, through the grasses and ferns and onto…

the space of white paper at the end of the roll.

It was time to say good-bye.

They cut the long strip of paper in two. Lila took one half
and Frannie took the other.

They knew that someday, somehow, they would join
the two halves and fill that last white space with color…
someday, when the two best friends were together again.